This book belongs to.......................

CONTENTS

Willowbank
Gift Book

Drawn by Carlos Busquets

PUBLISHED BY PETER HADDOCK LTD.
BRIDLINGTON ENGLAND
© PETER HADDOCK LTD.
Printed in Russia

A Foxy Lesson

The Summer holidays had arrived, and the Willowbank Glade schoolmaster, Mister Reader, prepared to close the school for the break.

"Now I want you all to be good while I'm away," he told Sundown and his friends. "When I come back you can tell me all about your holidays."

Six weeks later, it was nearly time to start
school again and one morning Sundown and
Rainbow were thinking about Mister Reader's
return when they spotted a stranger
approaching the village.

"It's a fox," said Rainbow. "They can be very
sly."

"I didn't hear the alarm," said Sundown. "The guards must be asleep."

"What shall we do?" asked Rainbow. "He might be a bandit."

"Yes, he looks very nasty," agreed Sundown. "Come on, let's get a rope."

Sundown was a clever squirrel and he quickly made a loop on the path, knowing the stranger would walk that way. Then, with all their strength, Rainbow and Sundown pulled the rope tight around the fox.

Unable to escape, the stranger was furious. "Let me go," he shouted. "I'm the schoolmaster in Willowbank."
Sundown and Rainbow were shocked.

"No you're not," said Sundown. "Mr. Reader's our teacher."

"Not any more," snarled the fox. "Untie me and I'll show you the letter Mister Reader has written and you naughty children can call me Sir ... Is that understood?"

Sundown released the fox and took him to
Grandfather Pen the badger. He read the letter
and seemed satisfied with the new
schoolmaster.

"I want you two in school very early
tomorrow," grumbled the fox. "I'll give you
some lines as punishment."

The next day, the Willowbank children were very unhappy at school. The fox made them work extra hard. They had to write a story about their homes and all the things that were in them.

"Leave nothing out," the fox reminded them. "It's important you write about every cupboard and drawer."

The hard work made Sundown sleep heavily that night. The following morning he noticed a group of villagers crowded around the old tree stump.

"That's right," Mrs. Long Whiskers was saying. "All my best acorns have gone ... And they were hidden in a special place."

School

"My best bottle of dandelion wine is missing," grumbled Mrs. Silver Quill. "No one but my son and I knew where that was stored."

It seemed most of the villagers had mislaid or lost something of value.

19

Sundown soon forgot about the gathering as Schoolmaster Fox made the children do their sums. Then the squirrel noticed something that was very puzzling.

"He's got that sum wrong," Sundown whispered to Rainbow.

Sundown was confused. Schoolmasters were supposed to be clever. They were not supposed to make mistakes over simple adding up.

At lunchtime, Sundown went to tell Grandfather Pen.

"I was worrying about him myself," said the badger. "There are some bad spelling mistakes in the letter he brought. Mister Reader would not have made silly errors like that."

Grandfather Pen made up his mind to have a
serious talk with the new schoolmaster. With
Sundown scampering behind, they went to the
school-house where the fox was having his
lunch.

And what a lunch it was!

22

"That's Mrs. Silver Quill's special bottle of dandelion wine," exclaimed Grandfather Pen.

"And I'm sure those are Mrs. Long Whiskers's acorns," added Sundown.

The table was sagging beneath the weight of food and valuables.

23

Of course, the fox was an imposter who had asked the children to write about their homes so that he knew the best things to steal.

It was not long before the guards were escorting the sly animal to the outskirts of Moonshine Wood.

"He won't come back again," smiled Grandfather Pen. "Everyone in the neighbourhood will know he is a bandit."

"What about Mister Reader?" asked Sundown suddenly.

"Goodness yes," nodded the badger. "The fox must have captured him on his way back to Willowbank."

A full search of the wood was made and at last they found the schoolmaster tied up in a remote hut. He was not hurt and before long he was back in the classroom … and he had a special word of thanks for Sundown.

Lost in the Snow

It was Winter in Willowbank, and many of the creatures had gone to sleep to avoid the cold. Sundown Squirrel had been born in the Springtime and knew nothing of icy winds or freezing snow.

Sundown had recently met a new friend. The young fox cub, called Number Three because he was the third one born that season, was great fun to play with even if he did live a long way from Willowbank.

As they raced amongst the trees and explored the countryside, Sundown and Number Three strayed deeper into Moonshine Wood. When they stopped for a rest the youngsters saw something white and wet falling from the sky. Before long, as the white rain settled they discovered a great new game.

Soon everything was covered in a thick
blanket of brilliant white and it was only when
the snow had stopped falling that the friends
realised they were totally lost.

The snow made things look very different and
as they looked about them, Sundown and
Number Three began to feel the cold.

On they trudged, trying to find a familiar landmark, and, as it grew colder, they wandered further into the wood. By the time they reached a wooden hut, the two friends were exhausted.

"Be careful," warned Sundown, sniffing the crisp air, his tail twitching rapidly. "I smell danger."

Number Three laughed at his friend's caution
and crawled through the hole at the bottom of
the door.

"All right," said Sundown, still nervous of the
hut. "You stay here. I'll try to get help."

Half an hour later, Sundown was shivering
with the cold and close to tears. Suddenly a
black shadow hovered above him.

There was a swoosh of beating wings, and Sundown closed his eyes in fear. Then a deep, hollow sounding voice said, "You silly little squirrel, what are you doing out here dressed like that?"

Sundown looked timidly up at the branch above him. There sat Lonely, the barn owl.

Lonely lived in a big tree on the outskirts of Willowbank and was a rather mysterious creature. He was called Lonely because when he was born he had no brothers or sisters.

"Come on," invited the owl. "Climb on my back, I'll take you home."

The strong bird swooped soundlessly through the trees towards Willowbank. Mrs. Brush Tail, Sundown's mother, made her son some hot soup and soon he was warm again. But Sundown was worried about Number Three.

"Grandfather Pen has agreed to help," said Mrs. Brush Tail as the wise old badger came into the room.

"That's right, young Sundown," said Pen. "You wrap yourself up in some warm clothes and we'll soon be on our way."

Sundown was happy that someone as important and clever as Grandfather Pen had decided to search for the fox cub.

"There really is nothing to worry about," said Grandfather Pen. "Lonely told me where he found you. From there we will follow your tracks."

Sundown discovered that it was easy to follow a trail in the snow, and it was not long before they reached the hut.

"What's wrong?" asked Sundown as Grandfather Pen stopped suddenly.

"That is a Cloud Head hut," whispered the badger. "They are big animals so tall that their heads are in the clouds. We try to keep away from them. They are strange creatures."

At last, Grandfather Pen was satisfied that the hut's owner was not around and they went to find Number Three.

Sundown looked inside, his nose working against the odd odours that rose from the strange objects in the hut.

"Number Three's not here," said Sundown, anxious to get to the fresh air. "Perhaps he's around the back."

Then, as Sundown squeezed through the hole
in the door, a familiar shout reached his ears.
"Coo-ee!" it said.

Next second, Sundown jumped with surprise
as something cold and wet sloshed into his face.

Slowly recovering from the shock, Sundown wiped the snow from his eyes. "What was that?" he asked.

"I think your friend Number Three has recovered," laughed Grandfather Pen. "I also think he has learned about snow while he's been here."

Sundown waited only to give the fox cub the warm clothing they had brought. Then the battle started.

With a smile, Grandfather Pen left the two youngsters to their game.

"Remember," he called back to Sundown. "You'll know your way home by the tracks in the snow."

But the two creatures did not hear the wise badger's words. They were too busy enjoying themselves.

The Naughty Weasels

One sunny morning Sandy Squirrel and his friend, Ronald Rabbit, were bored. Suddenly, they heard the sound of the town-crier's bell. They wondered what was happening.

The best way to find out was to go and listen. And so they did. The town-crier read the proclamation: The mayor will present a prize to the people who sweep and tidy their street in the shortest time.

44

Sandy and Ronald thought that this was a good idea and decided to take part. In any case, the streets were very untidy. Leaves and branches were everywhere.

The two friends collected their
brooms and a wheelbarrow and
started work at once.

They had to make a good job
if they were to win the prize as
everyone else wanted to win too.

Oh, dear! Just as the
competition was about to start,
who should arrive in town but the
wicked weasel gang. They
discovered that there was to be
a competition with a prize, so
they decided to enter.

Then battle commenced. The
weasels were really rather
lazy, but they worked quickly
because they wanted to win
the prize.

Sandy Squirrel and
Ronald Rabbit busily picked
up all the rubbish from their
street and took it to the tip,
which was rather a long
way away.

Because it was such a long
way to go, the two friends spent a
lot of time walking to and from the
tip. But they had to dispose of the
rubbish properly.

On the other hand, the naughty weasels
did not want to waste time by going to the
tip so they threw their rubbish into the first
place they found. They thought that
nobody would discover their dirty trick.

As you can imagine, they
finished their work very quickly. All
they had to do now was collect
the prize. "It doesn't matter that we
cheated," they said. "The main
thing is to win."

As Sandy and Ronald continued
working and taking their rubbish to the
proper tipping place, the weasels arrived
dancing with joy. "We have won the
prize," they shouted.

Grandpa Mole, however, was not sure
that they had done the job properly. He
wanted to check their work before the
mayor presented the prize.

The naughty weasels had tipped all their rubbish into the moles' den. They were very angry and threw it all back into the street.

When the weasels and Grandpa Mole
arrived, the street was even dirtier than
it was before the weasels began
cleaning it.

So it was only right that Sandy Squirrel and Ronald Rabbit won the prize for their hard work and honesty. As for the weasel gang, they had to sweep the streets for the rest of the year as a punishment for their dishonesty.

Flood Alert

Only the tinkling sound of the gently flowing stream and the buzz of a busy bee disturbed the peace as Sundown Squirrel and Rainbow Rabbit sat lazily in the warm sunshine.

"This stream once ran through Willowbank Glade," announced Sundown quietly.

Rainbow yawned, not very interested in the history of the village where the young animals lived.

"As Moonshine Wood grew," Sundown continued, remembering the story told to him by the wise old badger Grandfather Pen, "the stream became diverted."

"Good job too," laughed Rainbow. "Otherwise we'd get awfully wet!"

They began to doze again as a rhythmic gnawing sound lulled the young creatures to sleep.

CRASH! Suddenly there was a frightening noise. Sundown and Rainbow leapt to their feet as a shower of water drenched them. A stout tree had fallen across the stream.

61

Sundown was puzzled. The tree was not old or rotten and there was no wind. Then a high pitched chuckle came from the bushes. Next second, out popped a tiny, fidgety creature.

"Of course," said the squirrel. "It's Saw Tooth Shrew."

The three friends played happily, balancing and scampering across the fallen tree. Then the clouds grew black, the sun went in and it started to rain.

Willowbank Glade was some distance away,
so they decided it was time to go back to their
dry homes.

Two hours later, the rain was still falling
heavily. Normally the stream would have taken
the water away, but now, thanks to Saw Tooth,
it was blocked.

During the next three hours, the stream became a flood and tried to surge around the tree trunk. It found a new path and began to flow through Moonshine Wood.

Because of the rain, most inhabitants of the wood were in their homes, but a lone song thrush named Sweet Call had been to see a friend in the pine forest. She flew over the flood and realised the danger to Willowbank Glade.

Sundown and his two friends were the first
creatures Sweet Call met as she fluttered to the
ground. They were tired of sitting in their houses
and had come out to play in the rain.

Sundown realised at once that the fallen tree
had diverted the stream back to its original
course.

"The water will flow right through Willowbank again," he cried. "Can you imagine the damage it will cause. We must move that tree."

They hurried to the spot where the tree had fallen.

Sundown pushed, Rainbow pulled and Saw Tooth gnawed, but the tree would not move.

Then Sundown noticed that Saw Tooth was
shivering as if an icicle had gone down his
jumper.

"What's wrong?" he asked.

"Can't you smell it?" the Shrew stammered.
"It's a c-cat!"

Next second the three friends saw the creature approach. It was Swish Tail. Sundown and Rainbow knew the cat well enough to keep their distance, for he was a bad tempered individual. As for Saw Tooth ... cats simply loved to eat shrews.

Swish Tail, as usual, had been up all night. He was tired and grumpy as he tried to find a dry place to rest. At last he settled himself in the shelter of a bush.

Sundown thought about creeping off while the cat was asleep, but then he remembered the danger to Willowbank. What could move the tree trunk?

"If he was angry enough," whispered Sundown, "a big cat like Swish Tail could do it."

In a flash the plan had formed in Sundown's mind and he hurried to look for a strong vine.

Very carefully he wound the vine around the tree trunk and then, even more carefully, he tied the other end to the cat's tail.

All they needed to do now was startle Swish Tail awake.

With the screams of the three youngsters ringing in his ears, Swish Tail leapt to his feet to give chase. He hardly noticed the weight behind him ... until it became caught between two trees.

Swish Tail could do no more than howl at the
escaping animals as they raced back to the
safety of Willowbank.

With the tree removed, the stream reverted
to its correct course, and the flood never
reached Willowbank.

"We were lucky," Sundown said with a frown.
"But in future, Saw Tooth, be more careful which
trees you chew. Swish Tail may not be so helpful
next time."

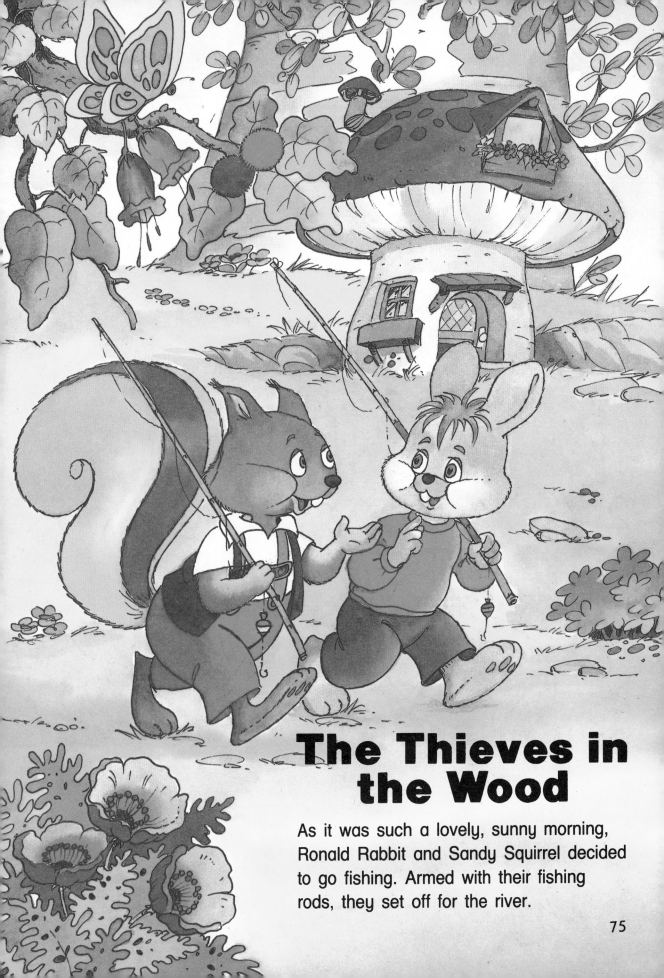

The Thieves in the Wood

As it was such a lovely, sunny morning, Ronald Rabbit and Sandy Squirrel decided to go fishing. Armed with their fishing rods, they set off for the river.

Suddenly, two little mice ran by as fast as their legs could carry them. They were very frightened of something.

Our two friends called to them but they kept on running in the direction of the village. Our friends wondered what had happened.

They soon found out! Two thieves had taken over the woods and had collected all the nuts and fruit which the villagers needed.

Ronald and Sandy protested. "The woods belong to everyone," they said. But the thieves, who were armed with big sticks, only laughed. "If you want fruit," they said, "you can have this." And they pelted our two friends with rotten fruit which had fallen to the ground.

79

Although they ran away as quickly as they could, our two friends still were hit several times with the rotten fruit.

Once they were in a safe place, they began
to plan a way to punish the two thieves.
But they needed to know where the stolen
fruit was hidden.

They climbed up a tree and, very carefully, jumped from branch to branch until they discovered where the stolen fruit was hidden. It was not easy to see.
The thieves had made a wooden hut and covered it with branches. On the door was a big padlock. They patrolled round it, armed with their sticks. They hoped that when the villagers became hungry, they would be able to sell them the stolen fruit and nuts.

Sandy and Ronald went back to their hiding-place in order to plan their next move. Ronald was a very clever rabbit and he soon thought of a way to recover the fruit and nuts.

He went at once to visit Mr. Mole and
told him of the plan. Mr. Mole agreed
to help.

He took our two friends through his
burrows until they arrived at the place
where the thieves had hidden the fruit.
Ronald made a hole under the hut with
his pickaxe and the fruit tumbled down
the burrow. Sandy picked it up and put
it in his basket.

The two thieves had no idea that our
friends were nearby. What a shock they
got when suddenly they were attacked
by flying fruit.

They took to their heels and ran away
as quickly as they could. It would be
a long time before they dared to come
back!

All the villagers celebrated because
the woods belonged to everyone again.
They were very grateful to our two
clever friends.

The Prize Bridge

One autumn morning Sandy Squirrel and his friend, Ronald Rabbit, were on their way to school. The summer holidays were over and it was time for them to concentrate on their lessons.

However, when they reached the stream the water was so high after the heavy rain during the night, that they could not get across it.

They were very cross because this was not the first time that it had happened. They had to think of a way to solve the problem once and for all.

Being very clever animals, they soon had a good idea. They would build a bridge which everyone could use. And without further delay, they started work.

Nearby were some fallen trees
which they could use for their bridge.
The trouble was, they were rather
heavy for the animals to lift.

The first log was almost in place when suddenly it began to move. In spite of the efforts of the two friends, it fell into the water with a big splash.

Unfortunately, Sandy and Ronald fell in
after it. Two weasels, who were also
on their way to school, roared with
laughter when they saw the plight of our two
friends.

"Enjoy your bath," shouted the first weasel. "You thought
you could build a bridge, did you?" asked the second weasel,
and still laughing they walked away.
Our friends were very upset because they had been so
excited about their idea. But, luckily for them, a kind
beaver was nearby and he decided to help them.

"We will teach those two weasels a lesson," he said. "I will help you to build the bridge, but don't tell them."

The beaver worked very hard and soon
he had lots of wood cut to the right size.
One of his friends happened to be walking
by and he stopped to help.

In next to no time the bridge was finished. It was really splendid. Our friends were very grateful to the beavers. They went on their way after our friends promised that they would not tell the weasels how they had managed to build the bridge.

Some time later, the two weasels returned after going the
long way round to cross the stream. They could not believe
their eyes when they saw the beautiful bridge. Mr. Badger
was walking by and when he saw the bridge, he too, was
amazed. "The teacher was worried because hardly
anyone went to school this morning," he said.

And, later that day, when they finally arrived at school, our friends were presented with a diploma by the teacher for their efforts.

The Fire Brigade

One morning, as usual, Ronald Rabbit and Sandy Squirrel went for a walk in the wood. They were sure that something exciting was going to happen.

107

Well, they were right! Poor Mrs. Rabbit was in trouble. Smoke was billowing from her house and she was shouting for help.

The two friends knew that they
had to do something quickly
because the fire was spreading.

They found a ladder for Mrs. Rabbit to climb down. Her neighbours had heard her cries and came to help too.

Everyone raced with
buckets of water and luckily
the fire was soon put out.
What a good thing that the
two friends were passing at
that moment.

When Mr. Badger heard what
had happened he congratulated
Ronald and Sandy. He told
them that he wanted to build a
fire-engine but he needed money
to buy the materials.

Our two friends immediately went
out with collecting boxes to try to raise
money for such a good cause.
Everyone was most generous except
the old mouse, who was very rich but
also miserly. "If my house caught
fire I would put it out myself," said the
mean mouse.

In spite of the mouse not giving
them anything, the two friends
managed to collect enough money
to buy what they needed to start
work on their fire-engine.

The mouse watched as they worked. "They only want our money because they like making useless things," he said.

All the other animals
refused to speak to the
mouse, so he thought of
plan to make our friends
look foolish.

He put some dry straw on a
plate and set fire to it. Then he
shouted for help.

When our friends heard him, they at once took their new fire-engine to his house and began to put out the fire.

118

They were really great. They
pumped lots and lots of water into
the house and the fire was soon out.

The mouse was
absolutely soaked
and his house was
so full of water that
it looked like a
swimming pool.

He was so ashamed of what he had
done that he apologised to the friends for
doubting their ability. As they were such
kind animals, they forgave him.

And to prove that he
really meant what he
said, the old mouse gave
our friends a lot of money so
that they could continue with
their good work.

THE END

CONTENTS